Throw-Away Pets

BY BETSY DUFFEY

Illustrated by Susanna Natti

A TRUMPET CLUB SPECIAL EDITION

To Alan and Paul

—B.D.

Contents

Throw-Away Pets

Urgent!

A note traveled across the classroom.

From Evie, to Will, to James, to Doug, to Tiffie, toward Megan.

Urgent! was written across the outside of the note.

Mrs. Hector was writing on the board. Her back was to the class. She was drawing the bones of the body.

Radius

Ulna

Patella

The other kids were writing. Evie was not. She was watching the note.

To Sasha, to Mark, to Sue.

Science was the only class that Evie had with Megan. She had been waiting all day to send the note. She had to let Megan know about her discovery. She hoped that Megan would read the note. She hoped that Megan was not still mad about yesterday. The note was almost across the room.

To Rachel, to Matt—

To Matt!

Matt held up the note and grinned. He opened the note and read it. Evie frowned at him.

"Now children." Mrs. Hector looked out at the class. Hector the Stricter. She had a kind of radar that could find anyone who wasn't paying attention.

Evie looked away from Matt to the front of the room and tried to look interested in what Mrs. Hector was saying. Would Mrs. Hector spot the note? It just had to get to Megan.

"There will be a test Thursday," Mrs. Hector said, "on the bones of the body. And, of course, tomorrow will be the science fair."

Matt dropped the note to his desk. His hand shot up. Evie froze. Matt wouldn't tell on her, would he?

"Yes, Matt."

"Joe and I are building a model of a rocket."

"Very good," said Mrs. Hector.

"Two stages."

"I said, 'very good,' Matt."

"It's the coolest rocket in the world and . . ."

"Thank you, Matt."

Matt shrugged and picked up the note again. He grinned at Evie. He held the note by two fingers and pretended that he was going to tear it in half.

Tiffie Sullivan raised her hand. She had seen the note. Would she tell?

"Janet and I are making purple celery," she said.

"Very good, Tiffie."

Evie stopped listening. She frowned at Matt. Would he ever stop causing trouble? That note had to get to Megan.

Three weeks ago when the science fair projects were assigned, Evie and Megan had decided to do theirs together. They decided to make a collection of different kinds of leaves.

Megan's part of the project had been to draw the cycles of photosynthesis on a poster. She had finished her part the first night.

Evie's part was to find the leaves for the collection. Evie had not done her part yet. She remembered their fight yesterday after school.

"You'll never get it done in time!" Megan had said.

"Will, too," Evie blurted out.

"Will not!"

"Will, too!"

"Evie? Will you tell us about your project?"

Radar detection!

Evie looked up quickly. Mrs. Hector's mouth was in a tight line.

"Oh . . . yes," said Evie. "Megan and I are making a leaf collection."

"Good," said Mrs. Hector.

Evie looked across the room at Megan. Megan was frowning at her. Megan's lips formed the words, "Will not," without making a sound. She was still mad!

Evie looked from Megan to Matt. She glared her most threatening stare at Matt. He winked at Evie but passed the note over his shoulder.

Megan picked up the note. She stared down at the paper, then back at Evie. Would she even open the note?

Megan unfolded the paper. Evie gave a sigh of relief.

As Megan read the note, Evie thought about the words that she had written:

Urgent! Meet me after school! Pet patrol emergency!

She had tried to make the note sound important. She had added fifteen exclamation points. No matter how mad Megan was about the science fair project, Evie hoped that she wouldn't ignore a Pet Patrol

emergency. Their club had helped a lot of animals. It was time to help some more.

Megan looked across the room at Evie. She didn't smile but she gave the thumbs-up sign to show that she understood and would meet Evie after school.

"Now class, we will move on to the muscles of the body," said Mrs. Hector.

Evie saw Megan take out a clean sheet of paper.

Evie did not take out a sheet of paper. She watched the big hand of the clock move slowly toward three o'clock. Toward the last bell.

"Come on," she urged the hand upward. "Come on!"

Big Trouble

*B*RRING!

Evie hurried out of the classroom door and waited for Megan in the hall. Matt and Joe came out first, grinning.

"What's so urgent, Evie?" said Matt.

"None of your business," said Evie. "You shouldn't read other people's *private* notes."

"It doesn't have anything to do with your science project, does it?" Joe asked.

"No," said Evie, "it doesn't."

"Well, just in case you think you have a chance to win first place, forget it," said Matt. "You don't stand a chance. We are building a rocket—the coolest rocket in the world."

"Right," said Evie.

"Two stages."

"I know."

"With a real . . ."

"*I know!*"

Joe punched Matt. "Come on," he said. "We got her mad." They laughed and whispered as they left the school.

Megan came out the classroom door.

"You won't believe it!" Evie called out as soon as Megan came into sight. "Follow me!"

Before Megan could even answer, Evie hurried down the hall and out the door of the school.

"Evie!" Megan called after her.

Evie stopped and looked back until she saw Megan was following her. Then she walked quickly to the bike rack and unlocked her bike. Megan caught up.

"Evie," she said, "what's so urgent?"

"Come and see for yourself." Evie jumped on her bike and pedaled down the street. Megan got on her bike and followed Evie. She rode up beside her.

"What, Evie?" said Megan. "What do you have to show me? We are supposed to be working on our *science* project! Did you forget?"

Evie didn't answer. She just pedaled even harder.

"Well!" said Megan. She tried hard to keep up.

They rode down the main street of town, then

turned behind an office building. Megan pulled her bike up beside Evie and stopped.

"It's due *tomorrow!*" she said. "We are supposed to be working on it right now!"

"Come on," Evie interrupted. "The science project can wait. We have all day to do the science project."

Evie put down her bike and walked over to a hedge at the back of the parking lot. She parted the branches and waved for Megan to come with her.

Megan did not move.

"Come on," Evie pleaded.

Megan still did not move.

"If you don't come, you'll never know what it is," said Evie. She stepped through the gap in the hedge. She waited on the other side of the hedge. After a moment she saw Megan ease through. She grinned at Megan. "I knew you'd come!" she said.

Megan frowned. "I'm coming," she said. "And this better be worth it!"

"It will be," said Evie.

Behind the hedge was a field. At the edge of the field stood a concrete block building. Until today Evie and Megan had never noticed the field or the small building. They were hidden by the hedge.

Megan looked at the building. On the front door of the building was a sign:

NO TRESPASSING

"If you think I'm going in there, you're crazy!" she said. "We could get into trouble, big trouble. We could . . ."

"Come on!" Evie called over her shoulder. She was already halfway across the field, running toward the building. Megan paused a moment, then ran after her.

They stopped together at the door. Megan tried to look through the wire mesh on the front of the door.

"What's in there?" she asked.

From inside the building came noises.

Rroww.

Ooooo.

Scratch. Scratch.

Megan's eyes got wider. Evie opened the door and the girls slipped inside. The door banged shut behind them.

Scratching noises came from the back wall of the building. As the girls' eyes got used to the darkness, they could make out a row of cages on the back wall. Most of the cages were empty. Three were not.

Rroww.

In the first cage, a large butterscotch-colored cat

paced back and forth. He had four white feet and white at the tip of his tail. He rubbed his head against the wire sides of his cage and began to purr when he saw the girls. A tag on the cage said JINX.

"A cat!" said Megan. "A cat named Jinx. Poor cat, locked up all alone!"

"There's more," said Evie.

Ooooo.

They turned to look at the second cage. A scruffy gray dog pressed his nose through the bars. His tag said WHEELER. One ear stood straight up; one pointed down. He peered out at the girls and howled. When he howled his whole body trembled.

"Poor Wheeler!" said Evie. His tail thumped when he heard his name.

Scratch. Scratch.

The scratching came from "Mr. C.," a white rabbit in the last cage. His bright eyes watched the girls as he stood and nibbled the straw in the bottom of the cage. The black spot on his nose twitched.

"A rabbit!"

For a moment the girls could only stare at the cages. "What's going on, Evie?" Megan finally asked. "What are these animals doing here?"

Evie shook her head and shrugged.

"I found them by accident," she said. "I was riding my bike to school. Flea was running along with me. We got to the office building and Flea stopped. He started barking and took off through the hedge." Evie's dog, Flea, was one of the four puppies the Pet Patrol had helped on its first job.

"He must have heard the animals," said Megan.

Evie nodded. "I followed him."

"He led you here?"

"Yes," said Evie. "The door was propped open then, but no one was here. Flea ran inside. I came in to get him out and found them."

"These are not wild things. These are pets," Megan said. "Who owns them? Why are they here?" She reached a finger inside the cage to rub the cat.

"Hmmm," Evie said. "Someone seems to be taking care of them. They have food and water. But something isn't right here. Pets should not be locked up like this. I think they need the help of the Pet Patrol!"

"I think you're right," said Megan. "But how can we help them?"

"I guess first we have to find out why they're here. Then we have to find out what we can do."

"Okay," said Megan. "Let's ask inside that office building. I bet someone there knows." She started toward the door.

"Good idea," said Evie.

Megan stopped and turned to give Evie a serious look. "But then we *have* to do our science project. Promise?"

"Promise," said Evie. She turned away from the cages and followed Megan.

Megan pushed on the door. It didn't budge.

Evie pulled on the door. Still it didn't budge.

Megan pulled harder.

Evie pushed harder.

As they pulled and pushed and pushed and pulled, Megan looked at Evie and said two words:

"Big trouble."

Trapped!

We're trapped!" Evie said. "It can't be locked! It opened when we came in!"

"It's only got a handle on one side," said Megan. "It's not made to open in this direction." She put her shoulder to the frame of the door and pushed with Evie.

"Now you've done it, Evie," she said as she pushed. "We're trapped. We're trapped in a building with a giant *No Trespassing* sign posted on the outside. How did I ever let you talk me into this one?"

Evie stopped pushing. "It won't budge," she said.

"How did you get out this morning?" Megan asked.

"The door was propped open."

"Now we know why!"

Evie paced around the small room. She pressed her face up against the wire mesh and tried to see outside.

"There has to be a way out," she said. "All we need is an idea."

"I've had enough of your ideas for today, thank you," said Megan. She sat down on the dirt floor and leaned against the wall. She crossed her arms.

"Maybe we can get out the windows?" Evie said. "Let's take a look."

Megan looked up at two high windows. "Well, okay," she said. She stood up. "Boost me up."

Evie made her hand into a stirrup. Megan stepped up and put her hands on the window ledge.

"Screens," said Megan. "Thick mesh screens. Screwed in." She stepped back down from Evie's hands. She sat back down on the floor.

"I guess we'll just have to wait for someone to come and let us out," Evie said.

"When will they come, Evie? What if we're trapped in here overnight?"

Evie shook her head. "Don't panic," she said. "We won't be trapped in here forever. The someone who has been taking care of these animals will be back sometime to feed them and give them water."

"How can you be sure?"

"Look, Megan, the rabbit's water bottle is almost empty. That means they'll be back soon."

Megan frowned. "Who will it be?" she said. "And what will they say when they find us in here?"

"Don't think about that," said Evie. "Let's think about something else."

Evie paced around the small room. She walked over to Jinx's cage. For the first time she noticed a clipboard on top of the cage. She picked it up.

"Look," she said. "Let's see what this says. Maybe it will tell us when someone will be back to feed the animals."

"Read it," said Megan.

Evie read from the top of the first page.

Douglasville Temporary Animal Shelter.

"This must be where the city keeps stray animals until they can take them to the big animal shelter in Minnistron."

"Maybe," said Megan. She got up and looked over Evie's shoulder at the clipboard.

"Look," said Evie. She ran her finger down a list of animals. "There were a lot more animals here. There are two kittens and three puppies listed in addition to Jinx and Wheeler and Mr. C. Beside each kitten and puppy it says *Sent to Minnistron.*"

"You were right," said Megan. "They must keep animals here that they find in Douglasville. Then they

take them to the shelter. But what about Wheeler and Mr. C. and Jinx? Why didn't they go?"

"Let's see," said Evie. "Here's Jinx."

She read from the clipboard.

"*Yellow cat. Male. Found April 27 at Green Acres Apartment Building.*"

Evie stopped.

She dropped the clipboard.

"What else?" said Megan.

"Nothing," said Evie.

"Then why do you have that funny look on your face?" Megan picked up the clipboard and ran her finger down the page until she came to the place where Evie had stopped reading.

"*Unadoptable,*" she read. "*Too old.*"

Megan dropped the clipboard. She looked at Jinx.

"Poor Jinx! You're not too old!"

Evie was already reading the gray dog's file.

Wheeler. Small gray dog. Found April 27 at the Quick Way truck stop.

Unadoptable—too old.

"No!" they said together.

Megan found the rabbit's line.

Rabbit, Mr. C. Delivered to shelter April 27. Unadoptable—too old.

They dropped the chart and stared at each other.

"I don't know what happens to animals that they call unadoptable but I have a feeling that it is not good," Evie said.

"I have the same feeling," Megan said.

"We need an idea. We need a great idea," said Evie. "We can't wait until the people come back. We need to save these animals now!"

Megan nodded. "We need your greatest idea ever! And we need it right now!"

Evie's Greatest Idea

Think, Evie. Think," Megan urged.

Megan picked up the clipboard. There was a pen attached to the top of it with a string. She turned to a blank page. "Just tell me all your ideas and I'll write them down." She held the pen over the blank page and watched Evie. "Well?" she said.

"I can't think of an idea just like that," Evie said, snapping her fingers. "It takes time to think of a good idea, and even more time to think of a great idea."

"Take your time," said Megan. "We need your *greatest* idea."

Megan wrote at the top of the page *Evie's Greatest Idea*.

"Okay," she said. "Ready?"

Evie was quiet for a moment. She stood up. She paced around the small room.

She looked at Jinx. *Rroww.* He called to Evie. He pressed his head up against the wires so that she could scratch him. His butterscotch fur was warm and soft.

"You're not too old," Evie said to him.

She looked at Mr. C. She touched his nose. It was cold. He wiggled it a few times. She picked up a piece of hay and stuck it through the wire. He nibbled at it.

"You're not too old, either," said Evie.

She looked at Wheeler. He moved toward the door of his cage. He licked the wire once and looked at Evie.

"You would be a great pet," she said to him.

He thumped his tail and barked once.

She had to think of something! She walked back and sat down by Megan. She gave Megan a serious look.

"Okay," she said. "Here's an idea. Call it: *Operation Jailbreak.*"

Megan began writing on the clipboard.

"We get out of here. We go back to our houses and wait until dark. After dinner, when our parents think that we're asleep, we sneak out and meet at the parking lot. We ride our bikes back here to the building and open the door."

"But we don't close the door," Megan interrupted, "because we know what happens when we—"

"Don't interrupt," said Evie. "Where was I?"

She thought for a moment, then continued.

"We open the door. We do *not* close the door. Then we open the cages and take out the animals one by one."

Megan kept writing.

"I carry Mr. C. You carry Jinx, and we bring a leash for Wheeler."

Megan nodded.

"Then we sneak them home and—*voilà!*—they're safe!"

Evie smiled at Megan, waiting for her reaction.

It was a great plan.

Megan didn't smile back.

"There's only one thing wrong with your plan," she said.

Evie frowned. "What?" she asked.

"The first part," said Megan. "The get-out-of-here part."

"Oh," said Evie in a small voice. "I guess you're right."

She thought some more. She got up and walked around the room one more time. Jinx purred. Mr. C. sniffed and scratched. Wheeler barked once.

She sat back down beside Megan.

"Okay," she said. "I've got another one. Write this down. *Operation Newsbreak.*"

Megan wrote it down. Then she looked up at Evie.

"Ready," she said.

"Okay, I learned this one from my mom," Evie said. "One time when my mom was in college, the college decided to cut down an old oak tree on campus to make room for more parking places. My mother chained herself to the tree so they couldn't cut it down."

"Your mom did that?" said Megan.

"Yes," said Evie proudly. "We'll chain ourselves to the cages. We'll refuse to move until these animals are saved!"

Megan waited. She was not writing this time.

"The TV crews will come. ABC. NBC. CBS. We'll get national coverage. *The Today Show. Oprah.* We'll tell the world! People won't stand for it and the animals will be saved!"

Evie stood with her fists in the air.

Then she put her hands down and looked eagerly at Megan.

"So, what do you think?"

Megan did not look too excited.

"Well," she said, "if we can't get out, how are we going to get the chains?"

Evie sat back down.

"Oh," she said. She put her head in her hands. She pounded her head a few times with her hands.

Then she looked up.

"I've got it! Write down *Operation 911 Rescue*."

Megan did not begin to write.

"Before I write this down," she said, "maybe I had better remind you that we don't have a phone."

"Oh," said Evie again. "That's right."

Megan grabbed Evie's arm.

"*Shhh*," she whispered. "Someone's coming. Listen."

Outside they heard the sound of footsteps coming toward the building.

Evie and Megan looked for a place to hide. The footsteps were coming closer and closer. The girls pressed their backs against the concrete block wall and watched the door. The sound of the footsteps became louder and louder. Someone stopped in front of the building.

Evie and Megan held their breath and waited for the door to open.

The Big Secret

*B*ang!

The door flew open.

"Matt!" Evie cried.

"Joe!" Megan cried.

Matt and Joe stood in the doorway. Matt's shoulder held the door open.

"How did you find us?" Evie asked.

Matt grinned. "We were suspicious about that note. We knew you were up to something, so we were spying on you!" he said. "We were just making sure that you didn't have a better science project than ours."

Evie tossed her head.

"Well, count on that," she said. "Flea could make a better science project than you guys."

"Just wait," said Matt. "We'll show you tomorrow. So where is it?"

"What?" asked Evie.

"Your project."

"What's back there?" asked Joe, trying to see over Evie's shoulder into the back of the room.

He turned to Matt.

"I think they're hiding their science project back there. Let's go see."

Rroww.

Ooooo.

Scratch. Scratch.

"Animals!" said Matt. "I thought your project had something to do with leaves."

He looked at the cages on the back wall.

"Animals?" Joe said. He stepped into the building.

"Wait!" said Evie. "Don't come in!"

Matt still held the door open with his shoulder. If he came in, the door would close!

"Don't move, Matt!" Megan called out. She held up her hands like a traffic cop.

"You can't stop us!" said Joe.

"No!"

Matt stepped forward a little and the door inched forward.

"Stop! Matt!" said Evie.

Matt grinned.

"You don't understand!"

Matt stepped in. The door swung forward.

Evie lunged for the door. Megan was right behind her. They reached for the door—

Bam! The door slammed shut.

"So what's the big secret?" said Matt, looking at the cages.

"The big secret," said Evie, "is that we're locked in here! That the door won't open from the inside."

"You're kidding!" said Matt. He ran back to the door. He pushed on the frame with his shoulder.

"Why didn't you tell us?" he said.

Joe came up beside Matt and helped him push.

"It's no use," Evie said. "The door is locked."

They turned to Evie.

"Now you've done it," Joe said.

"*I've* done it? It's *your* fault," Evie said. "You wouldn't listen. I told you not to come in."

Megan held up her hands. "This isn't helping," she said. "We don't need fighting—we need a plan. A plan to get out of here and to rescue these animals."

"Why?" asked Matt. "Why do they need to be rescued?"

"Look at this clipboard," said Megan. "It shows that this is a temporary animal shelter for the city. All the animals except for these three were taken to the big shelter in Minnistron."

"Why didn't they take these three?" asked Joe.

"It says they're too old."

"Too old?"

"What happens to them now?"

"We don't know," said Evie. "But we don't think it's good."

Matt nodded. "Well," he said. "It's a good thing I'm here after all. If anyone can figure it out, I can. Right, Joe?"

Joe looked doubtful.

"We've got to think of an idea to get out of here and to save these animals," said Evie. "Think, Matt."

Matt rubbed his hands together. "Don't worry," he said. "I've been known to have some pretty good ideas before."

"Right," said Megan, shaking her head. "Your ideas always seem to get you into trouble."

Joe smiled. "Like the time you hid the microphone in the teachers' lounge. That was a great one!"

Matt giggled. "Until the teachers found it."

"Or the time you put that fake vomit on Tiffie Sullivan's desk."

Matt giggled again. "Her face . . . how can I describe it?"

"You're not helping," said Megan. "We need an idea *now*."

"Okay," said Matt. "The brain is at work. Don't forget that Joe and I, animal detectives, solved the mystery of the trash cans last summer."

"The Pet Patrol solved that case!" said Evie.

"Well, we helped," said Joe.

"Okay," said Megan. "This is a new case. Think, Matt."

He picked up the clipboard. Where it said *Evie's Greatest Idea*, he marked out the word *Evie's* and wrote *Matt's*.

"Matt's Greatest Idea," he said, "coming right up."

He paused and looked at Joe and Evie and Megan. Then he shrugged and added, "As soon as I think of it."

Matt's Greatest Idea

Matt put his hand under his chin. He wrinkled his eyebrows. He twitched his nose.

"You look like Mr. C.," said Evie.

"I've got it!" he said.

"Okay," said Megan, "shoot."

"I saw this in an Indiana Jones movie," said Matt. "It's bound to work."

He signaled for them all to move in closer.

"Picture this: A man comes back to feed the animals. He walks in. He looks to the left. He see nothing. He looks to the right. He sees nothing. He looks straight ahead and . . ."

"He sees nothing!" said Evie and Megan together.

"So get on with it," said Evie. "Where have we disappeared to?"

Matt looked up at the ceiling. "We are hiding up on the ceiling." He paused for effect. "Then we jump him. We wrestle him to the floor. We grab him, tie him up, gag him, steal the animals, and make a run for it!"

Evie groaned. "That's impossible, Matt," she said.

"It worked for Indiana Jones," said Matt.

"How did Indiana Jones stay on the ceiling?" asked Megan.

"He held on to the rafters," said Matt. The four children looked up at the concrete ceiling. There were no rafters.

Evie shook her head. "Try again," she said.

Matt put his hand under his chin. He wrinkled his eyebrows. He twitched his nose.

"Okay," he said. "This time I've really got it."

"Shoot," said Megan.

"I saw this one in a Western. We just need some rope and a horse and . . ."

"Matt," said Evie.

"We tie the rope to the window . . ."

"Matt," said Evie, louder this time.

"We whistle for the horse."

"Matt!"

"What?"

"Where are we going to get a rope and a horse?"

"So, I don't have all the answers."

He thought some more.

"Now I've really got it. I saw this one in a prison movie. See, this guy was at Alcatraz. Life sentence. No hope of escape. Doomed to a life—"

"Just tell us, Matt."

"Okay," said Matt. "The guy had to escape through a vent with a screen covering it."

The four kids looked up at the thick mesh screen on the windows.

"So," Matt continued, "the guy stole a knife from the dining room. He used it as a screwdriver and every night when the guards were asleep he undid one screw. Then one night he undid the last screw, took off the screen, and escaped."

Matt looked around at Megan and Evie and Joe.

"Great!" said Joe.

"Great?" said Evie. "I just have one question."

"What?"

"Where are we going to get the screwdriver?"

"That," said Matt, "is the best part of the plan."

He reached into his pocket and pulled out his Boy Scout knife, and from the side of the knife he slowly unfolded a small screwdriver.

"Excellent!" shouted Evie. Megan and Joe cheered.

"Be prepared," Matt said.

He looked around the room. "Let's move one of those cages over here so that we can stand on it. Then we'll take turns undoing the screws."

Evie nodded. The four kids pushed one of the empty cages to the window.

"I'll go first," said Megan.

Matt and Evie boosted her up to the top of the cage. Slowly she stood up, keeping her balance against the wall.

She looked closely at the window. "Okay," she said. "Pass me the screwdriver."

Matt passed it up.

Megan started working on one of the screws. "This is going to take a while," she said.

Matt and Evie and Joe looked around the small room.

"I hate being locked up in here," said Matt.

"Now we know how they feel," said Evie, pointing to the cages.

"Hey, fella," Matt said to Wheeler. He turned to Joe. "Let's take him out of the cage."

"No!" said Evie. "Don't you dare open . . ."

Matt opened the cage.

Wheeler jumped out. He wiggled and rolled on the dirt floor on his back.

Matt laughed and scratched the little dog's chest.

Evie put her hands on her hips. "Put him back," she said, "or . . ."

"Freedom time," said Joe. He opened the cat's cage. Jinx jumped out and rubbed around Joe's legs.

"Nice kitty," Joe said. "See, there's no reason to keep them all cooped up."

"I'm warning you," said Evie.

"Come on, bunny." Matt opened the rabbit's cage. Out hopped Mr. C. Joe picked him up.

"Joe!" Evie said. "Keep the rabbit away from the cat! And the cat away from the dog. And the dog . . ."

It was too late.

Jinx spat. Wheeler growled. Mr. C. kicked hard with his back legs and jumped out of Joe's arms.

The animals raced around and around the small room.

Wheeler whooshed by Evie. She made a grab for him and fell onto the floor. She stayed in a kneeling position and tried to catch the animals as they scrambled around her.

A rabbit, a cat, a dog, then Matt and Joe.

A rabbit, a cat, a dog, then Matt and Joe.

Scratch, Rroww, Ooooo.

Matt hit the leg of the cage that Megan was standing

on. The cage swayed. Megan grabbed for the windowsill, then fell. Matt caught her as she fell. And they both fell against Joe.

On the floor was a pile of squirming kids, a growling dog, a kicking rabbit, a spitting cat. A pile of arms and legs and furry ears and wiggling tails.

In the commotion no one heard the sound of a truck driving into the parking lot. No one heard the footsteps coming toward the small building. No one heard the latch click.

Bang! The door flew open.

The Throw-Away Pets

A man stood in the doorway. He wore a tan uniform and carried a brown grocery bag. On his uniform was a badge that said: ANIMAL CONTROL—MR. BAKER. His mouth was open in a big circle.

He stared at the kids. They stared back.

Yip! Wheeler ran to Mr. Baker. Mr. Baker put down the grocery bag and picked him up. He scratched Wheeler behind the ears and stared at the kids. Finally he spoke. "Let's get these animals back where they belong," he said. "Then I have a few questions for you."

"I can explain everything," said Evie.

"Yes," said Matt, pointing at Evie. "*She* can explain everything."

Mr. Baker walked past the pile of kids to the cages. He opened Wheeler's cage and put him in. Matt carried Mr. C. to his cage. Joe took Jinx back.

Mr. Baker checked each of the animals. Then he turned and looked at the four kids. Then he smiled. "Now, what are you all doing in here?"

"It's a long story," said Evie.

"I have time."

Evie looked at the others then answered. "My dog, Flea, found the building this morning," she said. "He heard the animals and led me here. He went inside so I had to follow him in. Then I saw them." She pointed to the animals.

Megan cleared her throat. "Mr. Baker," she said. "Evie and I have a club, the Pet Patrol. Evie was worried about these animals. So she brought me here after school. When we walked in, the door closed behind us."

"We followed them," said Joe. "And we got locked in, too."

"I've tried to warn the city about that door," Mr. Baker said. "The owner of the office building out front lets the city use this place for free. It used to be a storage shed. That's why there isn't a handle on the inside."

"We just wanted to help the animals," said Evie.

"I understand you kids wanting to help the animals. But you know you shouldn't be in here," he said.

"It's not safe to go into unknown buildings. There could be something dangerous inside."

"And you might get locked in!" said Matt.

Mr. Baker laughed. Then they all laughed.

Matt looked at the closed door. "How are we going to get out?" he asked.

Mr. Baker smiled as he walked over to the door.

"The door's not really locked," he said, "just stuck." He reached up, slipped his hand into a crack above the top of the door, and gave a strong pull. It opened.

"We could have done that hours ago!" said Matt.

"You're free." Mr. Baker pointed to the open door.

Nobody left.

"Go ahead, kids. You can go."

Nobody moved.

Evie looked at the others, then back at Mr. Baker. "We have some questions, too," she said.

Mr. Baker paused for a moment, looking at the kids.

"Well," he said, "I guess you can stay a few minutes while I feed the throw-away pets but then you'll have to go. I have to close up for the night." He opened the grocery bag and began to take things out of it.

"Throw-away pets?" Evie and Megan said at the same time.

"What's wrong with them?" asked Matt.

"Nothing's wrong with these animals," said Mr. Baker. "Except that nobody wants them."

"Who threw them away?" asked Joe.

Mr. Baker poured dry food into the dog's bowl. He took out the water bowl and rinsed it out and refilled it.

"Well, take Wheeler here. That's what I named him. His owner left him on Highway 414 last weekend. Never came back for him. Some people don't understand how much work and responsibility there is in having a pet. They bring home a cute little puppy and pretty soon it's a full-grown dog that needs to be fed and walked. Then they don't want him anymore."

Wheeler barked at the water bowl in Mr. Baker's hand. Mr. Baker put it back in the cage and watched Wheeler drink. His tail thumped as he lapped up the water.

"What about this cat?" said Megan.

"Jinx?" said Mr. Baker. "Apparently thrown away when his owner moved to a new apartment. A lot of people think that a cat can survive in the wild."

Evie shook her head. "They can't," she said.

"They're not wild things. They're used to someone feeding them."

Mr. Baker nodded. He poured some cat food into the cat's bowl. "They don't know how to find their own food."

"What about the rabbit?" Matt asked.

Mr. Baker turned to the third cage and removed the water bottle.

"I'd guess Mr. C. only lasted six weeks in his home before he was thrown away. He was probably given to some kids for Easter."

He reattached the full water bottle and filled the small bowl in Mr. C's cage with rabbit food.

Megan looked up from Mr. C's cage.

"What do you do when you find them?" she said.

"First, I put an ad in the newspaper to try to find their owners in case they're lost. If no one claims them in three weeks, I take them to the big shelter over in Minnistron. I took a bunch over early this morning."

"But not Wheeler and Jinx and Mr. C."

"No," said Mr. Baker. "I'm afraid these are the ones that got left behind. These are the ones that were unadoptable. The shelter in Minnistron is crowded. They only take young puppies and kittens, and baby rabbits. That's what people want to adopt, not full-grown animals like Wheeler and Jinx and Mr. C."

"What happens to them now?"

"That's the worst part about my job," Mr. Baker said. "Tomorrow their three weeks are up, and tomorrow I have to take them to the vet to be put to sleep."

"No!" the four kids said at the same time.

"Yes," he said. "I'm afraid so. They can't live on their own, and nobody wants them. The shelter doesn't have room for them. We don't have a choice."

"Give us a chance," said Evie. "We can find owners for them. The Pet Patrol can do it. We found homes for four puppies one time in just one afternoon!"

"Older animals are different from puppies."

"Just let us take them."

Mr. Baker gave them a small smile. "I wish I could," he said. "But I can't just give animals away to children. Unless . . . would your parents come and sign for them?"

Evie shook her head. "My mother said no more pets for a year."

Megan shook her head, too. "I live in an apartment."

Matt and Joe shook their heads. "Remember when we took those two puppies home?" said Joe.

Matt nodded. "Our parents hit the roof."

"I tell you what, Pet Patrol," Mr. Baker said. He pulled a card out of his pocket. "I'll give you my phone number. You can have tomorrow to ask around and try to find homes for them. Call me if you have any luck."

Megan took the card. "You won't take them to the vet tomorrow?"

"No. I'll give you a day to work on it." He picked up the grocery bag. "Come on. I need to close up now."

He held the door open for them. Evie and Megan took one last look at the cages and followed Matt and Joe outside.

Mr. Baker waved as he got into a tan pickup truck and drove away.

Evie, Megan, Matt, and Joe walked toward their bikes.

Megan frowned and handed Evie Mr. Baker's card.

"It's hopeless, Evie," she said. "It's not possible to save them in only one day." Matt and Joe nodded.

"It has to be possible," said Evie as she watched

the truck pull out. From the building came the familiar noises:

Rroww.

Ooooo.

Scratch. Scratch.

"For their sake it has to be."

Say Yes!

The kids picked up their bikes. It was getting dark. Megan looked at her watch.

"I'd better get home," she said. "My mom will be worried."

"We better go home, too," said Matt.

They pushed their bikes forward. No one smiled.

"Call us, Evie," said Matt, "if you think of anything we can do to help them."

Evie nodded. She didn't answer. She could only think about the animals. They were alone now in the little building. Were they frightened? Were they lonely?

She rode with Megan toward home. When they came to a fork in the road, Megan waved and turned one way while Evie went the other. She rode on alone.

How could they do it? How could they find homes for Jinx and Wheeler and Mr. C.?

One time the Pet Patrol had had a sale to find homes

for four puppies. She shook her head. There was no time for a sale. And it would be hard to sell older animals.

Once they had dressed three puppies up in clothes and had left them on doorsteps. She shook her head. That wouldn't work, either. The animals were too big.

There must be a way. But what?

As Evie pedaled up her driveway, Flea came out and greeted her. He ran along beside her bike wagging his tail.

"Come on, boy," she called to him. He danced around her feet as she parked her bike and together they went up to her bedroom.

On the bed were the pieces of poster board for the science project. In all the excitement about Jinx and Wheeler and Mr. C., she had forgotten. Now it was too late. It was too dark to collect the leaves. Megan would be mad. Mrs. Hector would be mad.

She sighed. Even the greatest idea would not save her now. She had let them all down—Megan, Mrs. Hector, Jinx, Wheeler, Mr. C.

She put her head down on Flea's warm back. She couldn't imagine someone not wanting a pet, throwing it away like Mr. Baker said.

Pets *were* a lot of work. She had spent a lot of time with Flea, teaching him to come and not to bark at people. She fed him every day, walked him to give him exercise, and cleaned up after him. She took him to the vet when he needed shots and had to find someone to look after him when she went to the beach.

But he did things for her, too. He protected their house. He kept her company. He was always there to cheer her up when she was sad, like now. He loved her.

She closed her eyes.

A tear squeezed out from her eye and rolled down onto Flea's back. He turned and licked her face and whined.

"It's not fair," she said to Flea.

She thought of Jinx. His butterscotch-colored fur. His white paws and tail. And the way he purred when they patted him through the wire of his cage.

She thought of Wheeler pressing his nose against the wire cage. One ear up, the other down. His thumping tail. His soft gray hair.

And Mr. C. His bright eyes and the cute way he twitched the black spot on his nose.

If only people could *see* them. Anyone would want them for pets if they could see them.

Evie rested her head on Flea for another moment. Then she opened her eyes. She smiled.

"I've got it, Flea!" she said.

"*Yip!*" he answered.

Why hadn't she thought of it before?

An idea! A great idea! Evie's greatest idea!

She jumped up from the bed and ran downstairs to the phone. She pulled Mr. Baker's card out of her pocket and began to dial.

It was a great idea, but it would not work unless Mr. Baker said yes.

Say yes! she thought as she listened to the phone ring. *Say yes!*

The Science Fair

The gymnasium buzzed with the sounds of voices. Crowds of parents, teachers, and children had come to see the science fair.

Janet and Tiffie straightened rows of glass jars with purple celery sticking out of them.

Matt and Joe gave their rocket—the coolest rocket in the world—one last polish before blast-off.

Rroww.

Ooooo.

Scratch. Scratch.

Three cages were set up in the gym. On the wall behind the cages were posters with large black letters:

THE THROW-AWAY PETS.

The rest of the posters showed information that Mr. Baker had given to Evie and Megan. One told about the shelter in Minnistron and how it didn't have room to take older, "unadoptable" animals. Another poster told about picking out pets and about the responsibilities of owning pets.

The last poster was a sign:

THESE ANIMALS DESERVE TO LIVE

THESE ANIMALS DESERVE A GOOD HOME

DO YOU HAVE A GOOD HOME FOR

ONE OF THESE ANIMALS?

Students, parents, and teachers crowded around the cages.

Students, parents, and teachers petted the animals.

Mrs. Hector took Mr. C. out of the cage and passed him around. His eyes were bright. He twitched his nose at the children.

Evie held Jinx for the people to pat. They rubbed his soft butterscotch fur. He purred loudly.

Megan held Wheeler on a leash. He trembled with excitement as he looked at all the people. One ear pointed up, the other down. His tail did not stop thumping as the children patted him.

When the bell rang for school to begin, Evie and Megan put the animals back into their cages. Everyone

SCIENCE FAIR

THE THROW AWAY PETS

Inclined Planes and Screws

had patted them and held them, but no one had said anything about adopting them.

"This will never work," said Megan as they walked toward their classes.

"Will, too!" said Evie as they parted to go to their classrooms.

"Will not," called Megan, this time without her usual enthusiasm.

"Will, too!" called Evie. She hoped it was true.

They had stayed up late making the posters and getting ready. They got up early to meet Mr. Baker at the concrete block building. Matt and Joe had even come along to help them carry the cages. Mr. Baker brought them to school in his truck. He would be back at three o'clock to pick them up. Unless . . .

Evie tried not to think about it.

She met Megan at lunch to feed the animals. They took Wheeler for a quick walk outside and headed back to class.

But Evie couldn't concentrate on her work. She could only watch the clock. She thought about Jinx and Wheeler and Mr. C. Would anyone want them? The day was almost over and no one had claimed them.

Evie closed her eyes and put her head down on her

desk. She couldn't think about it anymore. They had done their best. It was up to other people now.

Brring!

Finally the bell rang for science class to begin. Evie and Megan and the rest of Mrs. Hector's class would go to the gym now to see all the projects. This was the last class of the day. This was the last chance for anyone to adopt Jinx and Wheeler and Mr. C.

Evie started toward the gym. *Will, too! Will, too!* Evie thought, hoping that it was true. Hoping that her greatest idea would work.

Will, Too!

Evie and Megan ran into the gym. They hurried over to their project. The animals were still there.

Rroww.

Ooooo.

Scratch. Scratch.

A blue ribbon was taped to one of the posters. Mrs. Hector walked over to Evie and Megan.

"Fine project!" she said. "Very thoughtful and educational. And I've enjoyed talking to Mr. Baker, too."

That meant that Mr. Baker had already arrived. Evie looked down at the floor. If Mr. Baker was here, then it was time for the animals to go back. They were out of time.

"And," said Mrs. Hector, "Mr. Baker has some good news for you."

Mr. Baker was walking toward them. He was smiling.

Suddenly, Evie felt hopeful again.

Maybe. Maybe, she thought. *Please. Please.*

"I have adoption certificates right here for Jinx and Wheeler!" Mr. Baker said. He unfolded the first paper. "Let's see," he said. "Jinx is going home with Dan Reinhold and Wheeler's new home will be"— he unfolded the second paper—"with Sasha Williams."

"Yeah!" Evie and Megan cheered. Matt and Joe hurried over.

"What happened?"

"Wheeler and Jinx have homes!" said Evie. The four kids jumped up and down and cheered. For once Mrs. Hector didn't even seem to mind the noise.

They opened the cages and let Jinx and Wheeler out.

Evie hugged Jinx. "I knew it!" she said. "I knew we could do it!"

Megan hugged Wheeler.

"That's not even the best part," said Mr. Baker. "The best part of all is this!" He waved a piece of paper in the air. "A waiting list—a list of people who want to adopt dogs and cats in the future. You girls should be proud of yourselves. I think the Pet Patrol has solved another case successfully!"

Evie smiled. She looked back at the empty cages. She was proud. Then she remembered the last cage. Mr. C.

He sat alone now. His bright eyes peered out from behind the wire. The black spot on his nose twitched.

Why hadn't Mr. Baker mentioned Mr. C.? She was afraid to ask.

"What about Mr. C.?" Megan said. "Isn't anyone going to take Mr. C. home?"

"No," said Mrs. Hector. "Mr. C. is not going anywhere."

The kids stared.

"He's not?" said Evie in a small voice.

"No, he's not," said Mrs. Hector. She opened the cage and took Mr. C. out. She handed him to Evie.

"Mr. C. is our new classroom pet!"

Evie hugged Mr. C.

Mrs. Hector smiled. "Mr. C., welcome to Riverwood School! And congratulations," she said to Evie and Megan, "for winning First Place in the science fair."

Matt and Joe looked at the blue ribbon. "First

Place?" Joe said. "What about our rocket—the coolest rocket in the world?"

"*Our rocket!*" said Matt. "We forgot to turn off . . ."

BOOM!

From the other side of the gym came the sound of a loud explosion. A shiny rocket streaked across the gym. On its tip was a piece of purple celery.

Matt, Joe, Evie, and Megan ducked under a table with Wheeler, Jinx, and Mr. C.

Mrs. Hector and Mr. Baker headed for the exit. Kids scattered in all directions.

Under the table, Matt began to giggle. Then Joe. Then Evie and Megan.

"I guess we won't be winning a prize this year," said Joe.

BOOM!

The second stage of the rocket exploded. The rocket zipped higher and came to rest inside the basketball hoop. For a moment the gym was quiet.

Then sounds broke the silence:

Rroww.

The sound of a very adoptable butterscotch-colored cat.

Ooooo.

The sound of a very adoptable gray dog.

Scratch. Scratch.

The sound of a very adoptable white rabbit.

And the sound of four voices calling out from under the table like a victory yell.

"Will, too!"

About the Author

Betsy Duffey is the author of the first two Pet Patrol books—*Puppy Love* and *Wild Things*—as well as other acclaimed chapter books like *The Math Wiz* and *The Gadget War* (both Viking). She lives in Atlanta, Georgia, with her husband, two sons, and two pets—Chester the dog, and Pete the guinea pig.

About the Illustrator

Susanna Natti has illustrated many children's books, including *Puppy Love, Wild Things*, the Cam Jansen mysteries (Viking), and the Lionel books (Dial). She lives in Bedford, Massachusetts, with her husband, two daughters, and one puppy named Jim.